PINK POLKA DOTS

A True Story about survival, because
sometimes, you don't have a choice.

Kathy Brooks Holloway

Cover design by:
Adam Grant/ Destiny Whitner

My sincere gratitude goes to my friends:

Ethel Lee
Irma Autler
Joyce Brown Geathers

For my children and
grandchildren-

I Love You All

Dedication

My Dearest Grandmother-

My Mother, no words adequately express the profound appreciation I feel for your immeasurable contributions to my life. I treasure each precious memory. Your boundless affection, unwavering support, and empathetic nature were blessings not only for me, but for all who were privileged to share your presence. Your fortitude and perseverance in the face of hardship has served as an unparalleled inspiration, shaping my character and imbuing me with strength. In moments of profound darkness, you were my steadfast anchor, my unwavering refuge, the one constant amidst the storm. Thank you for illuminating my path, for cultivating a love that will forever echo within my soul.

Pink Polka Dots

This story has been brought to life in film. This is further reading and acknowledgement to the screenwriter and actors who followed Christian Griffith's interpretation.

Cindy Lewis Smith- I am profoundly indebted to Cindy Lewis Smith. Her screenplay, *Pink Polka Dots*, masterfully adapted my novel, *Second Nature* into a work of art. Through "Red Lights," her song perfectly captures the spirit as it reflects my grandmother's thoughts. Offering a perfect melody which reverberates long past the film's ending.

Christian Griffith- Christian Griffith, the auteur behind the cinematic triumph *Pink Polka Dots*, invested his unwavering passion and unparalleled skill in its creation. The cinematography transcended all expectations. Its spectacular imagery was a stunning revelation, exceeding, even my wildest dreams. Griffith's painstaking craftsmanship transcended mere skill; it was a profound, almost

preordained fulfillment of his artistic calling. My sincere appreciation
extends to his family opening their home and hearts. Christian's
inherent drive and unyielding commitment to refining his vision of
Pink Polka Dots is simply awe-inspiring. He constructs the film as a
profoundly moving and deeply affecting cinematic experience. This is
truly a breathtaking achievement. Therefore, I offer Christian my
sincerest appreciation and gratitude that words cannot express.

Production Design - Kerri Brown, Eva Huntsman
Thank you, Kerri and Eva, for your hard work in bringing this film to life. You did the work of twenty that was not unnoticed.
Makeup Designers- Draven Marie, Emmie Wright A shout out for your
makeup expertise.
A special thanks to Keith Winchester of Winchester's Mufflers and More
located on McKinley Ave, in Frankfort, IN for the use of their cars in the
film which really made the experience of that era feel real.
Also, sincere thanks to Peddlars Alley Antiques who provided various props.

My heartfelt gratitude to the Actors who volunteered their time and brought Pink Polka Dots to life.

Kira L. Wilson- Pauline
Brenda Jo Reutebuch- Grace
Jeff A. Gossett- Didi
John Phipps- Melvin
Carolyn Strouder- Mrs. Peggy Sue Parker
Seth Hacker- Larry
Addison Grace Randolph- Mary
Blake Lee Goins- Dale
Rosalyn D'Amico- Janet
Danni Waters- Toddler Kathy
Lenox Rue Brannon- Baby Kathy
Micuylee Cheek- Nancy
Cindy Lewis Smith- Narrator
Kathy Brooks Holloway- Griever # 4
Charity Griffith- Griever # 2
Alvena Griffith- Griever # 3
Le Carol Goins- Griever # 1

FORWARD

My name is Kathy Brooks Holloway, and I bear witness to a tale that demands to be told. This is my family's history, a narrative etched in pain. Sharing this agonizing story of my life was difficult but needed to explain my grandmother's love, strength, giving the courage to me.

In a seemingly southern tranquil town of Hampton, Georgia, where the daily news rarely made national headlines, on January 4th, 1965 the upheaval that would soon shatter our peaceful existence happened.

My grandfather, Didi, a lumber mill owner, and my grandmother, Grace, of Cherokee Indian descent – a woman whose playful spirit provided a loving home for their only daughter, my mother, Pauline and her two siblings. Pauline, a vibrant soul ahead of her time, possessed a striking modernity. Her fashionable attire, always accessorized with beads and styled with Hollywood glamour, reflected her ambitious nature and bright outlook.

She yearned for a future filled with joy and family. My father, Melvin, was captivated by her radiant spirit, a captivating facade that concealed a darker truth. But Mary and Dale witnessed the truth with his scowls. I have no memories of these events. They are filtered through my older

siblings, Larry, Mary, Dale, and Janet.

Through their recollections, this story comes to life. Only through photographs, do I have a vivid portrait of my mother: her stylish hair, her jewelry, and her hats.

In January, I had not turned two, the day this traumatic unreal story begins; irrevocably altering the trajectory of our lives. My story is a testament to my grandmother's resilience of the human spirit, forged in the crucible of adversity. It's a narrative I share not only for my children and grandchildren but for all who seek solace in the face of unimaginable sorrow.

My hope is that this account will illuminate the enduring power of hope, the importance of self-acceptance, and the unwavering pursuit of peace and joy, no matter the darkness one confronts. The village of Hampton that raised me stands as a beacon of that enduring hope. A constant reminder that even amidst profound loss, life and love can flourish.

CHAPTER ONE

The click-clack of her heels echoed on the pavement as she strode purposefully from the courthouse, a brisk gait propelling her towards the large white house near the railway. The inviting porch spurred her slender legs to even greater speed; a snag in her new, expensive nylon stockings was a mere trifle on this momentous day. A radiant smile played on her lips, hope blooming in her heart. January 4th, 1965 – she was finally free from Melvin's grasp.

Melvin, the consummate charmer, the man who once seemed capable of captivating birds with his allure. But that was before his true nature revealed itself – a pattern of questionable employment. Only moments ago, in that stark courtroom, he had brazenly vowed that she would never receive one penny from him for child support as mandated by the court.

His furious exit sent a jolt through her, but now, the ordeal was over. She was nearly home. Her family and future await Grace, wielding a feather duster like a weapon in a playful skirmish with her daughters, didn't hear Pauline enter.

"I'll get you!" she shrieked, dust dancing in the sunbeams. Janet and Kathy, veterans of this game, giggled and dove behind furniture, seeking refuge in familiar hiding spots.

"Children! I'm home!" Pauline announced, her voice warm and resonant.

Grace chuckled, "You weren't supposed to see that, Pauline."

Pauline smiled, exuding a captivating radiance as she removed the hatpin that secured her stylish pink pillbox hat- inspired by Jacqueline Kennedy.

The afternoon light transformed her into an ethereal figure in the doorway, her dark hair framing her face.

Grace thought she looked like she belonged on a magazine cover in her pink polka dot dress. The children rushed to greet their mother, embracing her in joyous reunion.

"My darlings," Pauline murmured, her voice thick with emotion. "Oh, I'm so happy to be home." Pauline settled into her father's armchair with Kathy nestled on her lap.

Grace shed her cotton apron, collapsing onto the couch, her eagerness to hear the courthouse events palpable. "Children, why don't you go play, darlings, so your mother and I can talk," Grace said gently, ushering them away.

The children dispersed, leaving the two women to share the weight and the joy of their momentous day.

CHAPTER TWO

"It's finally over, Mother," Pauline declared, sitting erect preening her beautiful polka dot dress. The judge had finalized the divorce, and a child support order was issued for Melvin. His courtroom outburst fully displayed his rage as he cited to Pauline "you'll never receive a penny".

You can see Grace's concern as she gasped. Her fingers traced the cameo brooch at her throat. "Melvin's volatile nature has always been a problem," Grace responded, her head shaking in disapproval. "The sheriff should have put him in jail long ago."

She added, her voice firm with reassurance, "You and the children are safe here, darling. Your father will see to it. Melvin fears him, and rightfully so! I recall the day Melvin attempted to abduct little Kathy; I truly believed your father could have killed him then. Perhaps he should have."

A faint smile touched Pauline's lips, though apprehension lingered in her eyes. "Melvin certainly knows how to create drama," she murmured, her voice laced with weariness.

A courtroom spectator, an elderly woman

seated in the rear, witnessed the threat against Pauline. Terror etched upon her face, she let out a piercing shriek and fled the chamber, her frantic exit a testament to the gravity of the situation.

Grace, unconcerned, scoffed, "Some busybody, I imagine." Pauline, attempting to minimize her mother's anxiety, downplayed the incident. But Grace's unease was palpable. Her fingers, restless and agitated, flew over her current needlepoint project—delicate blue and yellow blossoms meticulously stitched onto a pristine handkerchief.

This familiar task soothed her frayed nerves. Replacing the embroidery hoop in its tin container, she donned her apron and resumed dusting, her movements deliberate and precise. "Mary will be relieved when she gets home," Grace stated, striving for optimism. "She always saw through Melvin."

Years ago, Pauline was married to Herman, father of her three children—Larry, Dale, and Mary.

Grace continued, her voice laced with worry, "Even before you married that brute, Melvin, Mary was petrified of him. Pauline revealed a chilling detail, "I found a knife hidden under Mary's pillow. She explained that she would protect me if she had to."

Grace paused, a thoughtful frown creasing her brow. "Where is Mary, anyway? She left hours ago, supposedly to visit Nancy. That girl is always up to something."

Pauline, leafing distractedly through a magazine, concealed a tear rolling down her cheek. "She'll be home for dinner, Mother. She always is."

Grace placed a comforting hand on Pauline's shoulder. "Now, darling, stop fretting. "A profound sense of relief washed over Grace; the divorce was finalized. Melvin was gone.

"I'm preparing dinner, Pauline. Your father's favorite—fried potatoes."

CHAPTER THREE

Eleven years old, and already the acrid tendrils of rebellion snaked upwards from the cigarette, mirroring the smoke curling above Mary's slight frame.

Nancy, her best friend since first grade, inhaled deeply, a harsh cough punctuating the stolen moment. The shared cigarette passed back and forth; a silent pact sealed in the twilight's hush.

Distant farm sounds – the rhythmic bark of dogs, the guttural groan of a tractor – formed a melancholic counterpoint to their clandestine ritual. Nancy's hesitation was palpable. Mary, attempting a veneer of nonchalance, whispered, "Mother won't even notice one missing."

The old barn, its paint peeling like sunburnt skin, offered a haven. The pungent aroma of hay and manure, a rustic perfume, battled the cigarette's cloying scent. Leaning against the slightly ajar door, Nancy gazed at the stacked bales in the shadowy loft.

Mary, adopting a preternaturally mature tone, declared, "It makes me look worldly, don't you think?" Striking a pose, one hand on her hip, the other elegantly holding the contraband, she aimed for an imitation of sophisticated glamour. "All the beautiful women in Mother's magazines smoke," she asserted, attempting to justify their actions. "I'm practically Audrey Hepburn!"

But Nancy's apprehension remained, a knot of fear tightening in her chest. "My mother will discover this," she warned, her voice laced with dread. "She'll banish me for eternity! Worse, she'll tell Dad, and I'll be grounded until the cows come home!"

Mary scoffed, dismissing Nancy's anxieties with a dismissive wave. "Don't be such a scaredy-cat!" she exclaimed, sprinting after Nancy as they fled the barn, their secret clutched tightly between them, a shared transgression hanging heavy in the fading light.

CHAPTER FOUR

Under the cover of twilight, the two young women attempted a clandestine entry through the rear entrance. Unseen, Nancy's mother, diligently preparing the evening meal, observed their furtive movements from the periphery of her vision. Nancy's query, "What's for supper, Mother?" was a guileless façade.

Mary, with practiced nonchalance, approached the sink, quenching her thirst and discreetly rinsing away the telltale aroma clinging to their clothes. "Those biscuits appear exceptionally scrumptious, Mrs. Parker," she offered, a transparent attempt to deflect attention from their lingering scent of illicit tobacco.

Mrs. Parker saw through the window the light was fading. She asked Mary, "Shouldn't you be getting home?" Her gaze darting to the darkened exterior through a cautiously parted curtain. Mary responds "No the lights aren't on. Mother said it's time to come home when the porch lights are on."

The absence of the light was a carefully chosen strategic observation. The antique telephone, a monstrous black behemoth residing on a living room table, emitted its jarring summons. Ring! Ring! The resonant peals sliced through the tense silence.

Both girls remained frozen, their mouths full of the incriminating biscuits, while Mrs. Parker, stirring the simmering stew, observed their deception with a steely gaze. "That apparatus won't answer itself, you know," she remarked pointedly.

Ring! Ring! With measured deliberation, she set down the spoon, wiped her hands on her apron, and, fixing on the girls with a penetrating stare, strode to the phone. "Hello?" A moment of hushed expectancy followed, then, a horrifying expression contorted Mrs. Parker's face. A hand flew to her mouth, stifling a cry of disbelief.

"Don't fret about Mary; she'll remain here tonight," she whispered, her voice laced with a strange mixture of fear and grim acceptance. The receiver was replaced with glacial slowness. The gravity of the news communicated by the phone line manifested in an immediate, frantic response, as she raced to the window, violently lowering the blind and bolting the front door.

She leaned heavily on the door, regaining her composure before returning to the kitchen, the weight of unseen horrors etched upon her features.

CHAPTER FIVE

Pauline devoured TRUE STORY, a ritual her father playfully mocked, questioning her bulk purchases. Each article captivated her; she lingered over every scandalous detail, finding them more sensational than any televised melodrama.

A gentle query drifted from her lips, "Do you need help with dinner, Mother?" From the kitchen, Grace's calm response echoed, "All's well, dear." The aroma of melting lard in the cast iron skillet spoke of comfort and tradition as the potatoes were frying. "I'm just so happy you're home." Grace's contentment was palpable; she was so happy that her daughter and grandchildren had.

The children reveled in the familiar warmth. Pauline knew, with unshakeable certainty, that this home would always be her sanctuary.

"I share your sentiment, Mother," Pauline replied, her voice imbued with heartfelt affection. "The children adore being here with you and Dad."

Janet and Kathy, engrossed in their dolls, returned to the living room. Kathy's yawns betrayed her exhaustion; sleep tugged at her eyelids. Pauline gently scooped up her drowsy daughter for a nap, carrying her to the sanctuary of her bedroom.

After tucking Kathy into bed, a tender kiss sealed the moment. Returning to the living room, Pauline sank back into the armchair beside the window, resuming her enthralling read, lost once more in the pages of her magazine. Janet, my sweet girl, come nestle close. Let me share one of my tales with you.

Abandoning her beloved doll, she snuggled into her mother's embrace. Pauline, her gaze lost in the fading light, turned towards the window. A breathtaking spectacle unfolded before her—a canvas of cotton-candy clouds, painted fiery hues by the departing sun.

With theatrical flair, Pauline commenced her story, her daughter snuggled contentedly against her. The narrative spoke of relentless training, of pushing physical limits to the brink of agony, a thrilling addiction disguised as gymnastics. Janet chuckled, a soft tremor in her chest, as her mother's embrace tightened.

Meanwhile, Larry, Pauline's firstborn, entered, a battery-powered lantern in hand, his tinkering in the backyard now concluded. The derelict car, a hopeless case, held an irresistible charm, a testament to youthful fascination. "Granny, have you any power cells for this antiquated light?" he inquired.

Pauline's mother directed him to the stash, adding a gentle reprimand about the screen door. His small transistor, blasting Atlanta's airwaves from his hip pocket, filled the kitchen with a cacophony that grated on Grace's nerves.

Unnoticed, a vehicle glided into the driveway, its engine hushed, its headlights extinguished before anyone could perceive its arrival. A shadow fell upon the scene, unseen, unheard.

Pauline, engrossed in a magazine story about a dashing, blond coach with captivating blue eyes, was jolted from her reverie. A thunderous blast shattered the peaceful scene.

The magazine flew, as Pauline threw Janet from her lap away from danger. Pauline jumped and started running from the door to get away from danger as he unloaded another round of buckshot on her. The searing pain of the buck shots peppered her hit her face, and chest.

Her pink polka dots left stained with blood across the wall. Through the window, a fleeting silhouette materialized: Melvin, her estranged husband, a shotgun clutched menacingly, his finger poised on the trigger. Another deafening explosion ripped through the air; Pauline collapsed, then sprawled onto the floor, crimson staining the pages of her story, her life ebbing away.

Grace's anguished cries for help pierced the silence from the kitchen, followed by Janet's frantic, barefooted escape into the enveloping darkness. She went through the briars and ended up at the neighbor's house.

Melvin, an unnerving calmness etched upon his features, strolled from the porch, leaving a trail of carnage in his wake. Larry, his attention momentarily diverted by the radio's jarring silence – the gunshot's roar swallowing the melody – experienced a sickening realization.

The crash of the lantern, as he startled, confirmed his dreadful suspicion. He saw Melvin depart, the chilling image etching itself into his memory. Dropping his tools, Larry sprinted toward the woods, as his step-father revealed in a heart-stopping moment.

Melvin, his gaze meeting Larry, swiftly reloading his weapon and training its deadly barrel on the young man retreating. A volley of buck shots erupted.

Larry staggered, and fell, and another blast found its mark. He tumbled, his body crashing into the roadside ditch. Melvin advanced relentlessly; the cold steel of the shotgun leveled at Larry's head.

The final shot echoed into the night. As Melvin thought he had sealed Larry's fate.

CHAPTER SIX

After divorce from her first husband, Herman, Pauline took a position in a bustling textile factory. Although Pauline was blessed with three lovely children—Larry, Dale, and baby Mary Ann which she took delight in. While Herman lacked Melvin's imposing physique, his temperament proved less volatile.

Their union dissolved, leaving Pauline to seek refuge with her parents in their home on Old Highway 3 in Hampton, Georgia. Then, fate intervened in the form of Melvin, the peddler. Tall, dark, and irresistibly charming, he captivated Pauline with his daily deliveries and flirtatious banter.

Initially, he displayed a feigned interest in her children, a deception quickly apparent to Mary Ann, who instinctively sensed his duplicity. She witnessed his contradictory behavior— offering sweets with one hand while his other conveyed a chilling disdain. Mary Ann implored her mother to reconsider, but Pauline, her heart ensnared, married Melvin. Their union produced two more daughters, Janet and Kathy.

However, Melvin's animosity towards Larry

and Dale was immediate and palpable. Perhaps it was the burden of raising another man's sons that ignited his resentment. Regardless, his hostility drove the boys back to their grandparents' haven on Old Highway 3. Mary Ann remained, bound by duty to her younger sisters and paralyzed by fear of Melvin's potential violence against her mother and siblings.

Melvin was a farmer and moonlighted in the illicit moonshine trade. His connections within law enforcement fostered a dangerous sense of impunity. His prolonged absences were punctuated by increasingly erratic and terrifying behavior upon his return. One chilling confession during a furious argument revealed a horrifying past: he boasted of murdering his first wife with a pitchfork and escaping then repeating that he would get away with it again. Their final Christmas together marked a brutal climax.

Infuriated by the children's innocent play, Melvin unleashed a torrent of rage, hurling his glass at the Christmas tree, shattering the festive scene into a thousand splinters of destruction and silencing the children's joyous cries. The act served as a terrifying culmination of the escalating violence that had defined their marriage. Pauline's request for aspirin ignited a furious outburst in Melvin. His rage erupted in a brutal strike, sending his wife crashing from her seat.

A welt bloomed around Pauline's eye, a stark

testament to his violence. With her children gathered, Kathy nestled in a baby buggy, a heartbroken Pauline embarked on the arduous journey back to their house on Old Highway 3, Hampton, Georgia – a retreat born not of choice, but of desperate escape.

CHAPTER SEVEN

Didi reveled in the joy of his grandchildren's company, a sentiment wholeheartedly reciprocated by the children. Atop the refrigerator, in a tin conspicuously placed yet playfully concealed, resided his treasure: a cache of peppermint candy canes.

The children, privy to its location, engaged in a delightful charade, their pleas for a treat a cherished ritual. Didi, a master of playful deception, feigned reluctance, prolonging their anticipation before finally granting their request. With a flourish, he'd mimic breaking each cane, the pretense of sharing a half-stick a charming ruse.

But the children, wise to his affectionate game, knew the truth: Didi, ever generous, ensured each grandchild received a whole striped delight, a testament to his boundless love. The Christmas at the Old Highway 3 residence, the following year, etched itself indelibly into his cherished memories. Pauline and her brood were gathered, a joyous assembly.

The Christmas tree, a magnificent specimen, towered over them, a fitting symbol of their abundant reasons for jubilation. Its shimmering lights cast a kaleidoscopic glow – ruby, emerald, sapphire, and amber – dancing across the walls and ceiling, a breathtaking spectacle. The aftermath of gift-giving was evident: a delightful chaos of discarded wrapping paper and scattered toys littered the living room floor.

Mirroring this vibrant scene was the infectious laughter and unrestrained excitement that filled the air, a stark contrast to the somber Christmas past. Grace, her mother, softly requested, "Pauline, darling, grace us with one of your songs; your voice is always such a treat." Pauline possessed a voice of exceptional beauty.

While she adored performing "Candy Kisses" and "Buttons and Bows," Christmas demanded her rendition of "Jingle Bells." This merry tune, sung in unison with her children, held a profound significance for her – it was the embodiment of unadulterated joy.

Dale, ever the showman, launched into the first verse, "Jingle Bells, jingle bells, jingle all the way..." Pauline's smile radiated as she joined him, followed by the children's enthusiastic chorus.

Her father, Didi, removing his pipe to beam, observed, "My heart swells seeing your happiness, my dear, and the children's delight." His voice carried a note of profound relief. "At last, Melvin's shadow no longer darkens your life. The upcoming court date on January 4th cannot arrive soon enough. We'll be free of that malignant influence forever."

CHAPTER EIGHT

The potatoes blackened, crisping to a cinder in the scalding lard. Pauline lay still, a crimson pool spreading beneath her on the floorboards. Her pink polka-dot dress, stiffening with dried blood, adhered to the wood like a gruesome decal. The cheerful yellow floral wallpaper was now a macabre tapestry, spattered with scarlet droplets and fragments of her torn clothing.

Grace, her hands slick with Pauline's lifeblood, knew the struggle was over. Helplessness, a crushing wave, overwhelmed her as she collapsed beside her daughter, a guttural scream tearing from her throat. Where was Janet? Just moments ago, the child had been nestled in her lap.

Perhaps hiding, Grace thought frantically, perhaps in her room. Maybe Larry would find her. Surely, he'd heard the carnage and would be racing home. The wail of sirens shattered the grim silence. Police cars converged, flashing lights painting the scene in strobing terror. An ambulance arrived, its doors groaning open.

Grace's heart hammered a frantic rhythm against her ribs. Still, no Larry. No Janet. Only the blessed, oblivious slumber of little Kathy, safe in her bed, a fragile island of peace amidst the storm.

The scene throbbed with chaos: the flash of lights, the blare of sirens, the grim faces of officers, and a throng of unfamiliar faces appearing from nowhere. An officer discovered Larry in a nearby ditch, clinging to life. He was rushed to Grady Memorial Hospital in Atlanta.

Janet was found at a neighbor's house. Her small body filled with thorns as she made her way through the briar patch. After brutally murdering his wife and thinking he killed his stepson also, he rode six miles outside of Hampton to a desolate dirt road where he ended his own life with a single gunshot.

The next morning, a procession of cars stretched a half-mile long on the driveway Mary noted as she approached home. Didi sat on the porch, rigid in his rocking chair, the rhythmic creak a futile counterpoint to the mournful cries echoing from within. He embraced Mary silently, as she approached the porch.

As his tears were streaming down his face, Didi was overcome with grief and could not find the words to say anything. For that, an overwhelming gratitude filled him. Inside, Grace was surrounded by a circle of grieving women. Mary approached her grandmother, the weight of the news settling upon her.

"She's gone, Mary. Your mother is dead," Grace whispered, the words a raw, searing pain. Her tears flowed endlessly, as the weight of the news was settling upon her.

Didi, overcome with grief went into the field knelt in the earth, raise his face up his anguished cry rising to the heavens pleading to God: "Why God? Why?".

CHAPTER NINE

In Jonesboro, at Georgia's Pope Dickson Funeral Home, Melvin and Pauline rested together, a heartbreaking scene. Their somber proximity—a horrifying emblem of a love brutally shattered— devastated the entire community and the children left behind. Kathy couldn't comprehend her mother's lifelessness. Didi, with agonizing force, finally detached Kathy's clinging arms from her mother's cold embrace.

Miraculously, however, Larry survived. His recovery, a protracted ordeal in the intensive care unit at Grady Memorial Hospital—the only Atlanta facility then equipped to handle gunshot injuries—was a testament to his resilience.

Finally, Grace welcomed her grandson home, her hands already overflowing with the immense task of nurturing five grieving children, orphans in the wake of their parents' brutal demise. Everyone felt the weight of their crushing sorrow.

Two months later, in the cruel irony on March 23, 1965, Grace dispatched her husband to the market for milk, a simple errand for little Kathy. As she washed dinner dishes, the kitchen window framing the railroad tracks paralleling Old Highway 3, catastrophe struck. A deafening roar shattered the quiet—the earsplitting shriek of metal on metal, the bone-jarring crunch of impact, the relentless rumble of a decelerating locomotive.

The cacophony seared itself into her memory, a haunting symphony of destruction. With the horrifying realization, she froze, and a dinner plate dropped from her hand as the shards scattered across the kitchen. No warning whistle pierced the night air.

Didi hadn't seen the approaching train at the overgrown corner opening. The train struck his truck, a brutal collision that dragged the mangled vehicle a mile down the tracks into the town of Hampton.

A mere two months after burying her beloved daughter, Grace was compelled to lay her husband to rest, the sole love of her life extinguished in a brutal instant.

CHAPTER TEN

The lumber mill, burdened by substantial debt, was rendered inoperable by Didi's absence. Unscrupulous debtors vanished, leaving Grace with no recourse but to sell the mill at a considerable financial loss. Drawing upon her husband's life insurance, she constructed a modest, three-bedroom dwelling for her grandchildren, a poignant location directly across from the railway tracks where her husband perished.

The piercing shriek of the train's whistle, though jarring, oddly provided Grace with a strange comfort; life, relentlessly, continued its course.

Larry, though eventually recovering from his injuries, bore the lifelong scars of profound emotional trauma. He joined the Army, finding solace in service. His physical and spiritual wounds healed overtime. He found love with Betty, a vivacious woman whose radiant spirit shone through her bright blue eyeshadow and playful mini-dresses.

A skilled cook and natural comedian, Betty brought a family of four children into his life, later expanding their family with twins, Paula and Pauline—a heartfelt tribute to their grandmother. Larry had a son with his second wife, his namesake. Larry lived a full life, passing away peacefully in 2003.

Dale, the ever-devoted brother to me, gently reassured his sister that she would always hold a special place in his heart, even as he prepared to marry Kathie Betty's cousin. I recall how he sought to reassure her with a tender, late-night conversation under the starlit sky, like I'd always be his girl.

A brotherly embrace meant to quiet any anxieties. Dale and Kathie had four children: Sophia, Tanya, Olivia, and Petrina. Dale and Kathie remain, to this day, residing in the home they built on their family's ancestral land in Hampton, Georgia.

Mary married young and produced a son named Michael. She found happiness with Rick Mancini. This wedding took place in a lavish Italian Catholic ceremony. They relocated to Connecticut, soon after the nuptials to be near Rick's parents.

Mary had a daughter, Michelle, with a wonderful man, Stephan Bowen. Tragically, the very cigarettes that had once saved Mary's life in 1965 ultimately led to her demise in 2008 from emphysema.

Janet embarked on a successful career as a Registered Medical Assistant (RMA), eventually ascending to the role of instructor. She is the proud mother of Ray and currently resides in Winston, Georgia.

Circumstances demanded Grace enter the workforce for the first time, taking a position as the head custodian at a Hampton elementary school. The relentless demands of the job, coupled with declining health and crushing stress, gradually eroded her vitality. A debilitating stroke ultimately claimed her life at the age of 68.

I was by her side as she peacefully passed, taking her last breath. I went into foster care after my grandmother's death. I then joined the Navy at age 17. I achieved the rank of Yeoman 2nd Class in the Navy.

I have an associate in science. An associate in business. A B.S., a M.B.A., and a B.N.D. I'm the proud mother of 3 children, Ashley, Casey, and Jack and two grandchildren Desi and Charlie. I currently reside in Winston, Georgia.

ABOUT THE AUTHOR: KATHY BROOKS HOLLOWAY

I was raised in Hampton, Georgia up until my grandmother's death. She provided a warm, stable, loving home. My grandmother, mother to me- was an exceptional human being.

She lit the way for me. Her strength inspired me. She left me too soon. My autobiography, Second Nature, served as a powerful emotional release, a conduit for processing the childhood trauma I endured. I hoped it would illuminate a pathway to healing for others, demonstrating that survival is possible.

My children's book, "Sometimes, I Do Not Like Hugs," aims to embolden young readers to articulate their feelings about inappropriate physical contact. The Georgia Department of Family and Children's Services adopted it for distribution to new foster parents, assisting children in identifying unhealthy relationships. "Sometimes, I Feel Afraid, Mad, Sad, and Confused" provides traumatized children with tools to seek support, embrace new experiences, and trust their intuition.

My accompanying activity journal encourages self-discovery, prompting children to explore their beliefs, experiment with different approaches, and consider alternative solutions.

This trilogy comprises a crucial resource for children and adults alike, facilitating essential dialogues around sensitive issues. It empowers adults to recognize and interpret a child's unspoken cries for help.

Finally, the film "Pink Polka Dots" is a heartfelt tribute, a visual expression of my profound gratitude for my grandmothers' unwavering love and inspirational influence.

Red Light Lyrics

Lyrics and music written by Cindy Lewis Smith
Performed by Cindy Lewis Smith & James Woody
for the Pink Polka Dots
soundtrack

RED LIGHTS- Cindy Lewis Smith

At the crossroads waiting for the train to pass
Wishing regrets would roll on down the tracks
Seems my heart remembers how its sad and frail
When it beats to the rhythm of the black steel
rails.

You dangled on a string in front of me
At the tips of my fingers where I couldn't reach.
Like a song I keep singing but it's out of rhyme
We were two step dancing to three quarter time.

You're a 20/20 vision when I'm looking back
I see the red lights flashing on the railroad track
I can't go forward, wish I could go back
If the train could take me I'd be where you're at.

You're a dream I remember but in black and
white I opened my eyes too late to realize. Now
the clock keeps ticking but the hands are still And
the world keeps spinning but against my will.

You're a 20/20 vision when I'm looking back
I see the red lights flashing on the railroad track
I can't go forward, wish I could go back
If the train could take me I'd be where you're at.

you're like a lonesome whistle blowing so mournful and low, You were always there, but where, I didn't know

You're like a 20/20 vision when I'm looking back
I see the red lights flashing on the railroad track
I can't go forward, wish I could go back
And if the train could take me I'd be where you're at.

I see the red lights flashing on the railroad tracks...
I see the red lights flashing on the railroad tracks
I see the red lights flashing on the railroad tracks If the train could take me I'd be where you're at.

Film Script

Credits

PINK POLKA DOTS

WRITTEN BY CINDY LEWIS SMITH FORMATTING BY LYNN HUBBARD SCREENPLAY

CO-WRITE/ EDITOR - KATHY BROOKS HOLLOWAY ADAPTED FROM SECOND NATURE BY KATHY BROOKS HOLLOWAY

DIRECTOR - CHRISTIAN GRIFFITH

PRODUCERS - KATHY BROOKS HOLLOWAY

CINEMATOGRAPHY - CHRISTIAN GRIFFITH

EDITING - CHRISTIAN GRIFFITH

PRODUCTION DESIGN - KERRI BROWN/ EVA HUNTSMAN

MAKE UP DEPARTMENT - DRAVEN MARIE /EMMIE WRIGHT

COSTUME DEPARTMENT - KATHY BROOKS
HOLLOWAY

VARIOUS PROPS PROVIDED BY - PEDDLARS ALLEY
ANTIQUES

NARRATIVE - RECORDED IN DONNY HAMMOND'S
AFTER DARK STUDIO- DALLAS, GA

SOUNDTRACK
Rock of Ages- Rosemary Siemens
The Prisoner's Song- Vernon Dalhart (1925)
Around the Christmas Tree- Elsie Baker (1914)
Mary Celeste- Keaton Henson
Little Christmas Shoes- Elsie Baker (1914)
St. Louis Blues- Bessie Smith (1925)
Starling Song- Kitty MacFarland
Red Lights- Cindy Smith & James Woody Recorded
at the Afterdark Studio (Cartersville, Ga) by Donny
Hammonds)

Actors

Kira L. Wilson- Pauline
Brenda Jo Reutebuch- Grace
Jeff A. Gossett - Didi
John Phipps - Melvin
Carolynn Strouder-Mrs. Peggy Sue Parker
Seth Hacker- Larry
Addison Grace Randolph - Mary
Blake Lee Goins - Dale
Rosalyn D'Amico - Janet
Danni Waters - Toddler Kathy
Lenox Rue Brannon - Baby Kathy
Micuylee Cheek - Nancy
Cindy Lewis Smith - Narrator
Kathy Brooks Holloway - Griever # 4
Charity Griffith - Griever # 2
Alvena Griffith - Griever #3
Le Carol Goins - Griever #1

Introduction-Main Characters (in order of appearance)

NARRATOR V.O. - Narrator is not scene on camera. Kathy is the youngest daughter of Pauline and Melvin. This is her story. She is a young woman,
approximately 18 years old, with a slight southern accent in her voice. The time is "now" but the story takes place in the 1960's in Hampton, Georgia.

PAULINE - Pauline is Kathy's mother, and the daughter of Grace and Didi. She is always well dressed, pretty in appearance and is a well-mannered southern lady. She has short stylish black hair, and her age would be around 30-35 years old.
She has a slight southern accent. She is married to Melvin.

GRACE - Grace is Kathy's grandmother and Pauline's mother. She is married to Didi. She and Didi own the large white house in Hampton, Georgia where most of the story takes place.

Grace is well dressed, wears her light colored, almost gray hair on top of her head swirled around with bobby pins, and speaks with a slight southern accent. She is in her mid-late 50's.

MARY - Mary is Kathy's 11-year sister. Her hair can be mid length with bangs and held back with a head band, she is wearing peddle-pusher pants, tennis shoes and socks, t-shirt and a light zip up plaid jacket. She should have a slight southern accent.

NANCY - Nancy is Mary's 11-year-old friend. She can be wearing her hair in a ponytail, dressed similar to Mary and other girls her age from the 1960's. She should have a slight southern accent.

NANCY'S MOTHER (Mrs. Parker) - She should be in her late 30's/early 40's. She wears a yellow printed day dress and an apron over the dress. Her hair is short, permed and pinned back on one side with bobby pins.

MELVIN - Melvin is Pauline's husband and Kathy's father. He should be close to the age of Pauline, approximately 35 years old. He is a stern looking man, blue collar worker, and he should look appropriate for the 1960's. He smokes cigarettes and has anger issues. Depending on the scene, he should look angry, and someone to be scared of.

DALE - Dale is Kathy's half-brother, Pauline's son. He is a pre-teenager, around 12 years old. Short hair cut as most boys in the 1960's. Clothing will depend on which scene, but always clean cut and well mannered.

LARRY-Larry is Pauline's oldest son. He is around the age of 14 years old. Short hair cut as most boys in the 1960's. Clothing will depend on which scene, but always clean cut and well mannered.

DIDI - Didi is Kathy's grandfather, His actual name is Elmer. Grace's husband and Pauline's father. He owns a lumberyard. He should look clean-cut, like a tough, strong statue of a 1960's man. Someone who loves his family, kind and gentle yet, he isn't anyone to mess with. He should be 55-60 years old.

Other Characters

HERMAN: he is Pauline's first husband, only appears in one scene. You will not be able to make out his features, but he will look different so that he is not confused with Melvin.

FRIENDS: middle aged adults, mostly women, who gather around Grace at her house after Pauline's death.

OTHER CHILDREN - All of Pauline's children are seen while walking to Grace's house. A total of 5 children oldest to the youngest - Larry (around 14 years old), Dale (12), Mary (11), Janet (3 or 4) and Kathy (2). Janet (in different clothing) is also seen sitting on her mother's lap at the window in the front room.

POLICE OFFICERS: present inside and outside Grace and Didi's house.

NURSE: she will be in the hospital room in a nurse's outfit from the 1960's, with a nursing cap.

NARRATOR: will be off screen. Speaking for Kathy as an adult.

Locations (SCREEN SETTINGS)

EXT: Of a Large white House in Hampton, Georgia, in the 1960's. The house has a big porch and a few steps to reach the porch from the walkway.

INT: of the Large white house, the living room. Needs at least a couch near the center, and a chair near the window. 1960's style furnishings.

INT: in a different house for the Christmas scenes; this can be the same living room in each scene, just with different furnishings.

INT: Nancy's house; scenes in the 1960's style kitchen and living room.

EXT: The yard outside the white house.

EXT: Walking area near a 2-lane road in the countryside.

EXT: a barn near Nancy's house.

INT: 1960's style Hospital room with equipment, hospital bed, monitors, etc...

PROPS

- 1960's decor and furniture

- baby clothing, old baby carriage

- 1960's model cassette player with microphone and a small transistor radio

- 1960's model police cars

- (at least 2) 1950/1960's model cars for Nancy's mother, cars passing on the road while Pauline is walking

- old vehicle in yard for Larry to be under the hood;

- 2 flowers one faded and one just like it in full pretty bloom to plant in the yard of the house

- Christmas tree and various different ornaments for decorations

- 1960's toys and dolls

- 2 replica newspapers - one for the Christmas edition, one for January 4, after Christmas

- Embroidery hoop and embroidery

- project/needle

- Peppermint sticks in a can, other foods, potatoes for Grace to peel

- cigarettes

- Feather duster

- dishes and glasses- one each that is ok with being broken

- A rotary dial phone for the living room scene.

- 1960's style hospital equipment and hospital bed 1960's TRUE STORY Magazines

- Shotgun

Other props as needed

PART ONE

FADE IN (EXT): On the sidewalk, the Camera slowly follows the footsteps of Pauline. We watch her shoes as she approaches her house. FADE OUT

FADE IN (INT): Inside the main house we see the grandmother, Grace, and 2 small girls (Kathy and Janet) who sit on the couch playing with dolls. Grace is dusting furniture, but stops and makes a funny face at the girls and starts dancing Native American style -like a Pow Wow - in front of the girls. The girls giggle and laugh. Grace uses the feather duster as part of her entertainment act. FADE OUT

FADE IN (EXT): The camera watches as Pauline climbs the steps to the porch and walks toward the door. Her coat swings open and we get the first glimpse of her pink polka dot dress. As the door opens, you can hear the squeaking of the old hinges and the heaviness of the door as it slowly opens.

INT: Pauline enters the house. She pauses as she silently watches her mother, Grace, dance around the room with the feather duster. The children are watching their grandmother, but when they see Pauline, they and run to their mother. Grace turns around and sees Pauline smiling at her. The children run and gather around Pauline.

NARRATOR V.O.:
This is my story. And if the story must be told, I might as well be the one to tell it.

INT: Camera is now on the two women. Grace puts down the feather duster and walks over to Pauline.

GRACE:
That was not intended for your eyes, Pauline! (She laughs a little) Pauline removes her pill box style hat and matching colored coat, tosses it on a near-by chair. Grace walks over to her daughter, Pauline, who is now holding the youngest child (Kathy) on her hip and another small child (Janet) at her feet.
Both women are well dressed, moderately. Grace is wearing a 2-piece matching dark colored skirt, white blouse and a gold brooch on her lapel. Her hair is high on her head and twisted around with bobby pins.
Pauline is wearing a form fitting pink polka-dot dress with a bow in the front at the waist. A flashy necklace adorns her neckline. Her short black hair

is 60's styled with high teased bangs and curls around her face.
Pauline is playing with the children as the Narrator talks.

NARRATOR:
Hampton is a small southern town near Atlanta, Georgia. My grandfather, Didi, owned a lumber mill there and made a good living. My mother, Pauline, was the apple of his eye. Mother had 5 children, Larry, Dale, Mary, Janet and me. I was the youngest. My name is Kathy. This is the day my story began, January 4th, 1965.

INT: Inside the house, main living room. The two women are talking to each other while the 2 children scatter off scene.

PAULINE:
Well, Mother, it's all over. The judge granted the divorce, and Melvin was ordered to pay child support. He made a horrible scene in the court room, stormed out saying that I would never live to see the day I would get a dime of his money.
Grace is shaking her head.

GRACE:
Melvin always did have a violent temper. The

judge ought to have locked that man up years ago. You and the children are safe here, honey. Your daddy won't let anything happen to you. You know Melvin is scared of that man and he has good right to be. That day he tried to kidnap little Kathy, I thought your daddy would kill him then. Probably should have.

Pauline almost lets out a little laugh, but still has a look of worry on her face.

PAULINE:
Melvin sure does know how to make a spectacle of himself. There was one older lady in the back of the court room that heard him threatening me. Why, she was so frightened for her own life, she practically screamed and got up and ran out. I don't know who she was. Just some busy-body I suppose.

Pauline is trying to make light of the situation for her mother not to worry.

Grace tries to busy herself by picking up the feather duster and begins dusting the furniture again.

GRACE:
Well, I think Mary will be happy when she comes home. You know, Mary has good instincts, she never did care much for Melvin. Even before you married him, Mary was afraid of him. Poor child,

she was always afraid he was going to hurt you or Janet and she had to be there to protect you, as if she could. Hummmpt!

No one could've stopped Melvin if he had a mind set to kill anyone.

Where is Mary anyway? She left here hours ago to run off to Nancy's house. That girl is always up to something.

PAULINE:
(Pauline is looking away from her mother now, trying not to show a tear in her eye, she is now thumbing through a stack of old magazines on the side table.)
She'll be along home for dinner, Mother. She always is.

GRACE:
(Grace stops dusting and puts her hands on Pauline's shoulders.)
Come on now, honey, quit your worrying. I'm about to fix dinner. You sit down and read your magazines.
I am making fried potatoes tonight, your daddy's favorite.

INT: Camera follows Grace into the kitchen as she puts on an apron, pulls out a bag of potatoes from under the sink and starts washing them in the sink to peel. FADE OUT.

FADE IN (EXT): Somewhere outside - Two girls, (Mary and Nancy) around the age of 11 are smoking a cigarette, leaning against the wall of an old barn in the country. You can hear a tractor plowing and dogs barking off in the distance. There is hay and farming tools inside the barn. The time would be around 5:00 in the evening. Mary is coughing.

MARY:
Mother will not miss just one cigarette, Nancy.
Mary passed the cigarette to Nancy and she takes a puff.

NANCY:
I think I'm going to smoke cigarettes all the time when I grow up. Don't you think it makes me look. more sophisticated, Mary?
Mary poses like a model from the pictures in her mother's magazines. Nancy passes the cigarette back to Mary who is coughing again as she inhales.
Nancy laughs at Mary when she poses with the cigarette.

NANCY:
What time is it? We better get back to my house before my mother misses us. She would ground me for the rest of my life if she caught me smoking.

Or, worse yet, she'd tell daddy and he would tan
my hide for a month of Sundays.
Nancy takes the cigarette back from Mary, inhales
one more time, then waves her hand in front of
her eyes to dismiss the smoke forming from
out of her mouth and tosses the cigarette to the
ground and stomps on it with her shoe.

MARY:
Don't be such a dork, Nancy. Nobody saw us doin'
nothin'.
The two girls run back to Nancy's house nearby.

EXT: Camera follows the girls as they run back
towards Nancy's house through a field, they slow
down when they reach the yard and calmly walk
through the back door as if they are innocent of
everything. Giggling.

INT: Nancy's house. In the kitchen, which is
entered through the back door.
Nancy's mother, wearing an apron, is setting the
table for dinner. We can hear the radio playing
from off scene. Nancy takes her regular seat
at the table. Mary stands near the sink, coughing,
takes a glass from the shelf and gets a drink of
water from the sink.

NANCY:

What's for dinner, Mama? Those biscuits sure look good.
Nancy's mother doesn't look up at either of the girls while she is busy.

NANCY'S MOTHER:
Mary, shouldn't you be getting on home right about now?
Mary takes a drink of water at the sink.

MARY:
No ma'am. The front porch light isn't on yet. Mother always says when the front porch light is on, dinner is ready. FADE OUT

FADE IN (INT): The phone is ringing. The camera is now on the black rotary dial phone on the side table in the living room of Nancy's house. The phone rings several times. FADE OUT

FADE IN (INT): Camera is back in the kitchen as Nancy's mother is standing over the sink wiping wet dishes with a towel.
We hear the phone ring off scene from the living room.

NANCY'S MOTHER:
That phone will not answer itself, you know.
Nancy's mother turns and
looks at her daughter Nancy, who is breaking small pieces off a biscuit on a plate in the center

of the table and doesn't look up at her mother.
The mother sets the dishes down, wipes her
hands on her apron and walks into the living room
to answer the phone. The camera follows her.
Nancy's mother answers the phone.

NANCY'S MOTHER:
Hello?
There is a long silence and her face turns
frightened.
Don't worry about Mary, she can stay with us
tonight.
She puts the receiver back on the phone in slow
motion. She stands for a moment, as in disbelief
of what she just heard. Then, she looks at the
front door and frantically runs to the door and
locks it. She runs to the windows and locks them
and pulls down the shades. She covers her mouth
with the cup of her hand and wipes away tears
that have formed in her eyes. Then she slowly
walks back into the kitchen. FADE OUT

FADE IN (INT): The living room of Grace and Didi's
house.
Scene picks up where it left off. Pauline is sitting
down in the chair by the living room window. She
is wearing the pink polka dot dress with the bow
at the waist.
Janet is playing nearby on the floor.

PAULINE:
How is dinner coming along, Mother? Do you
need my help?
Grace is off scene - heard from the kitchen.

GRACE (V.O)
 Just fine, Honey. It's so quiet and peaceful in this
house, even with you and the children here. I'm
just so glad you're home.

PAULINE:
Me too, Mother. The children love being here.
Janet, darling, come sit on your mother's lap. I'll
read you one of these stories from my magazine.
Pauline picks up a magazine from a table beside
the chair.

INT: Janet climbs into her mother's lap. The chair
is situated near the living room window facing the
front porch.

PAULINE:
*Pauline reads from the TRUE STORIES magazine, in
an exaggerated voice.*
If I wake up aching the next morning, it will be
because of my coach's exhausting routine. I love
my gymnastics class, but the launching, slamming
and squeezing my body past the edge of pain, is
addictive. FADE OUT

FADE IN (EXT): Outside Grace and Didi's house.
Tree frogs are heard off in a distance. Music is
playing off in the distance. The moon is full.
There's a shadowy figure of a man on the porch
staring into the window. Camera gets closer to
him.
A 12-gauge shotgun is pressed tightly against his
shoulder and his finger is on the trigger. FADE OUT

FADE IN (INT): Camera is back inside on Pauline
reading to Janet.

PAULINE:
My coach is a handsome, light-haired man with a
single lock of hair swaying across his eyebrows. He
has piercing blue eyes and a smile that...
A loud Gun shot is heard!

INT: Pauline is startled, she jumps up from the
chair, and Janet falls on the floor and starts crying.
We see Janet running towards the back. door
screaming.
Pauline turns around to see a glimpse of Melvin in
the window. FADE OUT.

FADE IN (EXT): Outside Grace and Didi's house on
the porch. The man quickly loads and fires
another shot through the window. FADE OUT

FADE IN (INT): We hear another gunshot, BUT -

Camera only sees the back of Janet's body as she's hit and falls to the floor. You can hear screaming and crying, glass breaking and pictures on the wall falling and crashing to the floor. The back door is heard slamming. We catch a quick glimpse of blood being spattered on the wall. FADE OUT

PART TWO

FADE IN (INT): December 25th, 1960, inside a smaller house (or different room) is a younger Pauline. She is wearing a different style hair do and dress with her 3 young children (Larry, Dale and Mary). It's Christmas time, a tree is up with decorations, lights, and the children are opening their gifts. The children are excited!
Wrapping paper is scattered across the floor. The children are in their pajamas opening their gifts. There is another man in the scene, Herman, Pauline's first husband, but he's off in a distance with his back turned and you cannot make out his face. He has a different color hair, shorter and skinnier than Melvin. Nicer disposition.

NARRATOR:
Although my story began on that eventful day, my Mother's story started much earlier. She was previously married to a man named Herman. They had 3 children together, Larry, Dale and Mary Ann. After they divorced, Mother met my Father, Melvin. Melvin was a peddler who delivered milk, produce and honey to my Mother's house.
FADE OUT

FADE IN (INT): A few years have passed-December

25th, 1962 DIFFERENT CLOTHING on everyone. Inside the house, with a little older Pauline, Melvin, same children- but they look older now, and 2 smaller babies. It's Christmas time, a tree is up with decorations, lights, and the children are opening their gifts. The children are excited! Wrapping paper is scattered across the floor. Melvin is sitting, slumped into a chair. He has a cigarette in one hand and he is drinking from a mason jar.

NARRATOR:
My grandmother, Grace, would say Melvin could charm the feathers off a chicken, and so my mother took a likin' to him. After they were married, my sister Janet and I were born. It wasn't long after that, that my father's true colors began to show. He was mean, abusive and just downright scary at times.

INT: Continuing the same scene from previously inside the house. Melvin stands up and starts yelling at the children, throwing the glass mason jar at the Christmas tree. It crashes, some of the ornaments fall to the floor and break. The children start crying, Larry and Dale stand up and take the smaller children to their bedroom for protection. Janet runs back to grab a doll that Melvin just kicked across the room. Larry quickly grabs her and takes her out of the room. Janet is crying.

Melvin continues to yell and kick the unopened Christmas gifts across the floor.

Pauline stands up, starts to argue and say something to Melvin and we see him swing his arm out, as if he's going to hit her. The camera doesn't see it if he does or not. Voices may be silent as scene is only shown, if necessary. FADE OUT.

FADE IN (EXT): Pauline and the children are walking on the side of the road. It's a nice summer day in rural Georgia. Pauline is wearing dark sunglasses, lifts them for a second, and the camera can see she has a black eye. She is pushing a baby carriage filled with overflowing clothes. The camera follows a baby dress as it slips from the carriage and falls to the ground. It goes unnoticed and is stepped on by the children. The older 2 children are carrying the 2 smallest children.

All are walking at a fast pace and trailing somewhat behind their mother. A car or two is seen driving by and passing them. One car blow's its horn at them. Pauline looks back at the children walking a little slower behind her, trying to keep up.

NARRATOR:
My father used to run moonshine. He once told my mother that he killed his first wife with a

pitchfork and had got away with it. He told her, if he had to, he would do it again. Mother eventually found the courage to leave him and take us kids to live with our grandparents. All that mattered now was that we were safe. FADE OUT.

FADE IN (INT): December 25th, 1964 Inside the GRANDPARENTS house. This time, with Pauline and her parents and the children. It's a happy scene. It's Christmas time. The girls are dressed in frilly holiday dresses and the boys are in dress pants and white collared shirts.
Pauline is wearing a light blue dress and matching shoes. The children are on the floor around the tree, 1960's Christmas music is playing and the grandparents are in living room chairs.
Didi has a newspaper in his hands he is reading. Grace has an embroidery hoop with fabric in it but lays it beside her as she is watching the children as they open their gifts.
Dale finds a gift with his name on it and he opens it. It's a cassette recorder.

DALE:
Mother! I love this tape recorder! Thank you very much!

LARRY:

Dale. Let me see it.
Larry stands up and goes over to Dale. Looks at
the cassette recorder.

LARRY:
I've seen ones like this before. Here, Dale, let me
show you how to put the batteries in it.
Larry opens the package of batteries and helps
him put the batteries in the tape recorder.

LARRY:
You put the cassette in it like this. Now, push this
button to record and this button to stop.

MARY:
Larry, can it record Mother singing?

LARRY:
I'm sure it can! Mother, you want to give it a try?
The children get excited and cheer on their
mother to sing.

PAULINE:
Oh my goodness, children! What would you like
me to sing?

MARY:
Jingle Bells!

Larry takes the recorder to Pauline.

LARRY:
Mother, hold this microphone in your hand like this, put it close to your mouth, and Dale will push the button when you're ready. This is going to be so neat!

PAULINE:
Are you ready? When do I start?
The children shake their heads yes and Pauline fumbles with the microphone.
Pauline begins to sing.

PAULINE:
(singing) Jingle Bells, Jingle Bells, Jingle all the way, oh what fun it is to ride in a one-horse open sleigh. Oh, jingle bells, jingle bells, jingle all the way, oh what fun it is to ride in a one-horse open sleigh.
The children join in singing.

MARY:
Didi? Can Janet and I have a peppermint stick?

Didi is sitting in an easy chair, reading the newspaper, he makes a funny frown at Mary, and pretends to hide behind the newspaper.

MARY:
Pleeeeeze, Didi?
Mary makes a pleading face at her grandfather and praying hands.

Didi smiles and winks at Mary and puts the paper down, gets up to walk into the kitchen. The smaller children get up and hurry to follow him. The camera follows them. He reaches up on top of the refrigerator and pulls down a colorful red and white tin can with a pop-off lid. Janet is tugging on his pant leg begging for a peppermint stick.

DIDI:
Who wants a peppermint stick?
The children squeal with excitement as Didi breaks the sticks in half and hands one to each of the children. The camera follows the children and Didi back into the living room.

GRACE:
I always love it when you sing, Pauline. You should do it more often.
Pauline turns and smiles at her mother.

PAULINE:
Maybe I will.

DIDI:
I am happy to see the children enjoying themselves. At least you don't have to worry about Melvin now. That man best not be trying my wits anymore. Come January 4th, everything will be over, and we can be rid of him for good.
Didi picks up the newspaper and starts reading it

again. The camera gets close and scans the date on the newspaper in his hands. It says December 25th, with a Christmas day headline. The children continue to play with their Christmas gifts in the background. FADE OUT.

FADE IN (INT): Inside the Grandparent's house, in the living room. The camera is on the (different) newspaper that is lying on the table beside the chair where Didi was sitting. We can read the headline of the newspaper, "January 4th". The page shows after Christmas sales. The Christmas tree is down. Room is staged as in the first scene from part one. *** THE SAME SCENE FROM PART ONE IS CONTINUED IN THIS SCENE WHERE IT LEFT OFF.

INT: The camera watches Grace is in the kitchen, same apron she put on in the first scene in part one, peeling potatoes in the sink. FADE OUT

FADE IN (INT): The camera is now back in the living room. Pauline is dressed in the same pink polka-dot dress with a bow around the waist from the first scene in part one. She is sitting in the chair by the window reading from a TRUE STORY MAGAZINE to Janet who is sitting on her lap.

PAULINE:
Are you sure you don't need any help, Mother?

Grace is off scene heard from the kitchen.
Pauline's lap and she is reading from the magazine
in an exaggerated voice.

PAULINE:
Now, where was 1? If I wake up aching the next
morning, it will be because of my coach's
exhaustive routines. I love my gymnastics class,
but the launching, slamming and squeezing my
body past the edge of pain, is addictive... FADE
OUT

FADE IN (EXT):
Pauline's VO still reading from the magazine.
PAULINE: (V.O. quickly from inside the house) My
coach is a handsome, light-haired man with a
single lock of hair swaying across his eyebrows. He
has piercing blue eyes and a smile that.... FADE
OUT

EXT: It's not completely dark outside yet. The faint
sound of music playing from a radio in the
distance, the camera watches as a car pulls
up near the driveway. Dust is blown up from the
road. The moon is full and rising. The brake lights
come on. The car stops. You can't see who's
inside the car. In the distance you can see a young
man with his head under the hood of an old car.
There's a dim light hanging from the top of the
opened hood. The young man - Larry appears to

be working on the car. He doesn't see or hear the car in the road. Only in the shadows, you can see a man open the door of the car and walk up towards the house and go up the steps. He is holding a shotgun at his hip. For a few seconds he watches through the window. Then slowly, he aims his gun and shoots through the window.

LOUD GUN SHOT.
Screams are heard as he reloads his gun and shoots through the window again.
FADE OUT.

FADE IN (INT): Scene cuts to Pauline's lifeless, bloody body face down on the living room floor. Spatter of blood nearby. FADE OUT

FADE IN (EXT): Outside, Melvin walks off the porch and walks through the yard heading for the dirt road where his car is parked. Larry, Pauline's oldest child, is outside, under the hood, tinkering on an old car engine when he hears the shooting. There is a transistor radio on the fender of the car playing music.
Larry drops his tools in hand and takes off running towards the house. Melvin sees him, reloads the shotgun and fires at Larry. Larry is hit twice with buckshot and falls to the ground. He rolls into a nearby ditch and pretends to be dead. Melvin isn't satisfied, reloads and walks over to Larry. He

stands over his motionless body, stares for a moment, aims and shoots him at close range in the head.

Convinced he is dead, Melvin walks aways. Melvin's face is without emotions. He walks to his car, gets inside and the camera watches his taillights as he drives away and dust is scattered from the road. The camera fades out to the moon, and the rising dust. The music from the radio is heard. Camera focuses on the radio still playing in the moonlight on the fender of the car Larry was working on. FADE OUT.

PART THREE

FADE IN (EXT): Outside the Grandparents home. It's the next day, morning.
The camera is focused on a lone daffodil or any flower-drooping - in the yard. The morning sun was shining behind the flower. We can see several police cars in the driveway and parked along the dirt road. The red lights on top of the cars are on and flashing.
The camera then clears and is focused on the porch of the house, where Didi is sitting in a rocking chair. He is wiping his tears away with a handkerchief. You can hear his gentle sobbing. Nancy's mother's car pulls into the driveway behind a police car. The camera watches as Mary, who is in the front passenger seat, doesn't wait for the car to stop completely before she opens the door and jumps out. She frantically runs toward the house. She pauses for just a few seconds to stare at her grandfather on the porch, their eyes meet, then she slowly continues through the front door. We can hear the heaviness of the door creak as it opens.
The Camera follows Mary inside.

INT: Mary stops as she sees fragments of her

Mother's pink polka-dot dress on the wall. Camera gets a closer look at what Mary is seeing. It's as if her mother's blood has glued the fabric to the wallpaper. Camera scans back to Grace, who is seated on the sofa in the middle of the living room. Several people (Grace's age) are gathered around her in a circle. One lady is holding her hand. Most are crying.

NARRATOR:
Mary didn't know that sneaking out of the house to smoke a cigarette that night, probably saved her life. After my mother was shot, my sister, Janet, got up and ran out the back door. She was so frightened that she didn't stop until she fell into a briar patch. I don't know how long she stayed there until someone found her.

INT: Camera is on Grace in her circle of friends, and moves behind the silhouette of Mary. We can only see the back of Mary's body standing looking at her grandmother. Mary isn't moving. She is in the center of the scene. Soft talk is heard in the background. Whispers from the ladies on the couch with her grandmother. The ladies are looking at Mary with sad and compassionate faces.
Grace is crying, wiping her eyes with a handkerchief, looks up and is speaking to Mary in the room.

GRACE:
Mary Ann, your mother is dead.

INT: The camera gets a close up on Mary's shocked face. There are tears in her eyes. She doesn't move or say a word. FADE OUT.

FADE IN (INT): Scene has moved to the inside of the Grady Memorial Hospital room.

NARRATOR:
My father left Larry for dead, but somehow he survived. He was taken to Grady Memorial Hospital in Atlanta and eventually recovered from his gunshot wounds.

My father got into his truck and drove away that night. He drove six miles south of Hampton onto a deserted dirt road. Then, he stepped out of his truck, reloaded his gun and shot himself. Georgia State Troopers found his body scattered along the side of the road an hour after he killed my mother. Both my mother and father lay side by side in Pope Dickson's Funeral Home in Jonesboro, Georgia.
They had to pull me off my mother's dead body, crying. All I remember is the smell of roses.

FADE IN (INT): Larry is unconscious and in the hospital bed hooked up to medical machines. It's quiet, except for beeping and heart beats sounds are heard. Camera scans the heart monitor first, then over to Larry and broadens to see the nurse in the room caring for Larry. The nurse is taking his pulse on his wrist and she's looking at her watch on her other hand. FADE OUT

FADE IN (INT): Grandparents home in the kitchen. Grace is washing dishes. It's a peaceful afternoon, the radio on the counter is playing some soft instrumental music on the radio station. Grace is humming with the music. We watch Grace wash the dishes. Didi comes into the kitchen to kiss his wife goodbye.

NARRATOR:
Two months later, my grandfather, Didi, had went to town for milk. He didn't hear a whistle blowing at the tracks and was struck and killed by the train. Without my grandfather, my grandmother lost the lumber yard.

INT: We hear the train wheels screeching, and what sounds like a car crash. We see Grace looking startled, she turns down the dial on the radio, and has a frightened look on her face.

INT: Grace drops the dish in her hands and in SLOW MOTION. The camera follows the dish to the floor and it breaks into several pieces. FADE OUT

FADE IN (EXT): Outside of the house, beginning with the front door and the camera moving slowly outward, towards the yard. The camera focuses on the one daffodil or flower in the yard that is now in full bloom. The sun is shining behind it, as the narrator continues.

NARRATOR:
I'm not telling you this story for sympathy. I'm not looking for your pity. But, for those who did not die, life went on. And, the rest of my story is about survival, because sometimes, you don't have a choice.
FADE OUT

THE END

Whatsoever things are true,
whatsoever things are honest...
whatsoever things are lovely...
think on these things.

PHILIPPIANS 4:8

www.ingramcontent.com/pod-product-compliance
Lightning Source LLC
Chambersburg PA
CBHW051308250626
47155CB00009B/3490